SCOUT
and ACE
TALKING TABLES

Written by Rose Impey
Illustrated by Ant Parker

Once upon a time, our heroes,

SCOUT and **ACE**

set out on a trip

into outer, outer-space.

Sucked through a worm-hole . . .

to a strange, new place,

lost in a galaxy called Fairy Tale Space.

"What shall we do?" says Scout.
"Let's try this place," says Ace.

But when Scout and Ace get there, the space café is closed.

No one is there,
just some tables
and chairs.

On one table there's a sack.
Inside it is a loaf of bread.
When Ace takes a bite . . .

. . . "Owww!" howls
the bread.

. . . but not on that chair!

Then the sack joins in.
"Put that bread back,"
shouts the sack.

Scout shouts, "Let's run for it."
"Let's take the sack," says Ace.
"And the bread as well."

"Help! Help us!" the bread and the sack both yell.

Scout and Ace race off.

But the table and chair race
after them.

Scout and Ace race past
a lorry and a bus.
"You'll be sorry . . ." warns
the lorry.

" . . . if you don't listen to us," adds the bus.

But Scout and Ace race on,
with the table and chair still
racing after them.

They race past a signpost.

The signpost grabs Scout
and Ace.
"Hello, hello. Who goes there?"

"Stop them," shout the
table and chair.

"Well, why didn't you say?"
asks the table.
"You sit down," says the chair.
"And tell us all about it."

Then their new friend the signpost brings them sausage and mash.

When it's time to go, the signpost points the way back to the SuperStar.
Scout and Ace wave goodbye.

"Chairs that walk!" says Ace.
"Tables that talk!"
"Who on Earth will believe
this?" says Scout.

Scout and Ace can't
wait to get out of
this crazy place.

"Here's a good one," says Ace.
"Where should you park a
spaceship?
On a parking meteor!
Boom! Boom!"

Scout groans. "Definitely time we were going!"

Fire the engines...

and lower the dome.

Once more our heroes...

are heading for home.

Enjoy all these stories about

SCOUT and ACE

and their adventures in Spac

Scout and Ace: Kippers for Supper
1 84362 172 X

Scout and Ace: Flying in a Frying Pan
1 84362 171 1

Scout and Ace: Stuck on Planet Gloo
1 84362 173 8

Scout and Ace: Kissing Frogs
1 84362 176 2

Scout and Ace: Talking Tables
1 84362 174 6

Scout and Ace: A Cat, a Rat and a Bat
1 84362 175 4

Scout and Ace: Three Heads to Feed
1 84362 177 0

Scout and Ace: The Scary Bear
1 84362 178 9

All priced at £4.99 each.

Colour Crunchies are available from all good bookshops, or can be ordered direct from the publish
Orchard Books, PO BOX 29, Douglas MM99 1BQ.
Credit card orders please telephone 01624 836000 or fax 01624 837033
or email: bookshop@enterprise.net for details.

To order please quote title, author and ISBN and your full name and address. Cheques and posta
orders should be made payable to 'Bookpost plc'. Postage and packing is FREE within the UK
overseas customers should add £1.00 per book. Prices and availability are subject to change.

ORCHARD BOOKS, 96 Leonard Street, London EC2A 4XD.
Hachette Children's Books, Level 17/207 Kent Street, Sydney, NSW 2000.
This edition first published in Great Britain in hardback in 2005. First paperback publication 2006.
Text © Rose Impey 2004. Illustrations © Ant Parker 2005. The rights of Rose Impey to be identified as
the author and Ant Parker to be identified as the illustrator have been asserted by them in accordance with the
Copyright, Designs and Patents Act, 1988. A CIP catalogue record for this book is available from the British Library.
ISBN 1 84362 174 6   10 9 8 7 6 5 4 3 2 1
Printed in China